A TEMPLAR BOOK

Produced by The Templar Company plc,
Pippbrook Mill, London Road, Dorking, Surrey RH4 1JE, Great Britain.

This edition produced for Parragon Books,
Unit 13-17, Avonbridge Trading Estate, Atlantic Road, Avonmouth, Bristol BS11 9QD

This book contains material first published in
Enid Blyton's Sunny Stories
between 1926 and 1953.

Illustrated by Angela Kincaid

Printed and bound in Italy

ISBN 1 85813 603 2

Enid Blyton's

POCKET LIBRARY

LOOK OUT, BUSY-BODY!

Illustrated by Angela Kincaid

‖ ·PARRAGON· ‖

Busy-Body the elf was always poking his nose into everything. He knew everyone's business, and told everyone's secrets. He was a perfect little nuisance.

He peeped here and poked there. If Dame Twig had a new hen, he knew all about it. If Mr Round had a new hat he knew exactly what it was like, and where it was from. He was a real little busybody, so his name was a very good one.

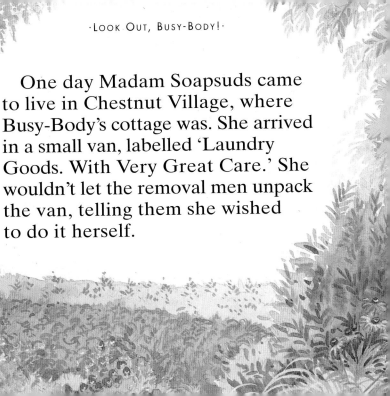

One day Madam Soapsuds came to live in Chestnut Village, where Busy-Body's cottage was. She arrived in a small van, labelled 'Laundry Goods. With Very Great Care.' She wouldn't let the removal men unpack the van, telling them she wished to do it herself.

Busy-Body was very curious, of course. Why should she want to unpack the van herself? Was there something magic in it that she didn't want anyone else to see? He decided to hide in the front garden, and watch till Madam Soapsuds took out whatever was in that little van.

That night, before the moon was up, Madam Soapsuds came out into the garden, and went over to the van. But before she opened the door, she

said a little magic rhyme:
"If anyone is hiding,
They must go a-riding,
On this witch's stick."
She tossed an old broomstick onto
the floor. Though he tried to escape
it, it swept poor Busy-Body out from
behind the bush where he was hiding,
and carried him up into the air,
feeling very frightened indeed.

"Ho, ho!" said Madam Soapsuds.
"I had an idea you were trying to

poke your silly little nose into my business, Busy-Body. Better stay away from me. I keep my secrets!"

So, while Busy-Body rose high above the village, Madam Soapsuds quickly and quietly unpacked that secret little van, and nobody saw her. Busy-Body had a dreadful night. It was windy and cold. He wasn't used to riding broomsticks. It was most uncomfortable, and very jerky, so he had to cling on tightly. He felt sure

the stick was jerking on purpose.
   When the sun came up, the
broomstick landed, leaving
Busy-Body stiff, cold and
very angry. How dare
Madam Soapsuds treat
him like that! He'd
find out all her
secrets, no
matter what!

Madam Soapsuds told everyone what had happened and they laughed. "How do you like riding at night?" they teased.

Busy-Body scowled. He hoped no one would like Madam Soapsuds. But they did like her, and very much too. She ran a fine laundry. They could take a bag of washing to her in the morning and have it back, washed, mangled, dried and ironed at tea-time. It was really wonderful.

She wouldn't let anyone watch her at work. "No," she said, "I like to work alone, thank you."

"She's got some special magic secret at work," said Busy-Body to everyone. "She couldn't possibly do all that washing herself. Why, she had seven bags of dirty linen to wash today, and a pile of blankets from Dame Twig. And hey presto! By tea-time they were all clean, dry and ironed!"

Busy-Body puzzled day and night over her secret. It might be magic machinery, or hundreds of tiny imp servants that had been in that van.

Madam Soapsuds had a big room in her house that nobody went into, called her Washing Room. Strange noises came from it, clankings, splashings and bumpings. "Can't I just peek inside and see?" asked her friend, Dame Twig. But Madam Soapsuds shook her head.

"No. It would be dangerous. Not even I go into that room. I just shake the dirty linen in there, shut the door and leave it. At tea-time I open the door, and there it is, clean, dry and ironed, piled neatly for me to take."

"Extraordinary," said Dame Twig. "Well, Madam Soapsuds, watch out for Busy-Body. He'll poke his nose into that room if he possibly can."

"He'll be sorry if he does," said Madam Soapsuds.

Busy-Body certainly meant to find
out the secret of that Washing Room.
He watched Madam Soapsuds from
the window of his cottage opposite,
every day. He knew that she did not

often go out during the week, but on Saturdays she went to visit her sister in the next village for the whole day.

"That's the day for me to go to her house," thought the elf. "She's away all day! I can get in through her window, because she always leaves it a little bit open. Oh ho, Madam Soapsuds, I'll soon know your secret and tell everyone! I'm sure it's one you're ashamed of, or you wouldn't hide it so carefully !"

That Saturday, Madam Soapsuds put on her best bonnet and shawl as usual, took a basket of goodies, and caught the bus to the next village. Busy-Body waited until the bus had left. He crept out of his cottage, and went round to the back of Madam Soapsuds' house. No one was about.

The sitting-room window was open as usual. He slid it up, and jumped inside. From the Washing Room he could hear curious sounds.

Slishy-sloshy, splish-splash-splosh.
Creak-clank, creak! Flap-flap-flap!
Drippitty, drip! Bump-bump-bump!
He stood and listened to the noises,
filled with curiosity. He must peep
inside and see what was happening.

The door was shut tight. He turned
the handle and the door opened.
A puff of steam came out in his face.
Busy-Body carefully put his head
round the door, but he couldn't see
a thing because it was so steamy.

He listened to the odd noises. Whatever could be making them?

He went cautiously inside. The door slammed shut behind him. Busy-Body turned in fright and tried to open it. But he couldn't! Ooooh!

The steam cleared a little, and he saw that the room was full of tubs of water, swirling steam, mangles that swung their rollers round fast and creaked and clanked, and hot irons that bumped their way over tables on which clothes were spreading themselves ready to be pressed.

No one was there. Everything was working at top speed by itself. The soap in the tubs made a tremendous lather, the scrubbing-brushes worked hard, the mangles pressed the water from clothes, the whirling fan that dried them rushed busily round and round up in the ceiling.

Busy-Body felt scared. He had never seen so much magic at work.

He felt himself pushed towards one of the tubs. In he went, splash, into the hot water. A large piece of soap ran over him and a big frothy lather appeared. He spluttered as soap went in his eyes and nose.

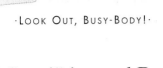

"Stop! Stop!" begged Busy-Body.
But the magic couldn't stop. It was
set to go, and go on it had to.
Besides, it didn't often have a real
person to wash, mangle and iron!

Poor Busy-Body was soaked in tub after tub, soaped and re-soaped, lathered, and scrubbed till he felt as if he was nothing but a bit of rag.

He was whizzed over to one of the mangles whose rollers were turning busily, squeezing the water out of the flattened clothes. Look out, Busy-Body!

He just managed to fling himself down below the mangle before he was put in between the rollers.

He crawled into a
corner, and wept.
Why had he
bothered about
Madam Busy-Body's
horrid secret?
A tub rolled near him, splashing
him with cold water. Then he was
flung up to the ceiling, where he
was hung on a wire to dry in the
wind made by the magic fan, and
then thrown back down to the floor.

Look out, Busy-Body! You are
near the magic irons! Wheeeee! He
was up on the ironing table, and a
hot iron ran over his leg! Busy-
Body squealed, and leapt off the
table. Into a tub of hot water he
went this time, and a big
scrubbing-brush began
to scrub him in delight.
Then he was flung into
a tub of cold water
and rinsed well.

"I've never been so wet in my life! I've never had so much soap in my mouth and nose and eyes! Oh, how can I get away?"

It was lucky for Busy-Body that Madam Soapsuds came home early that day, or he would certainly have been mangled and ironed sooner or later. But suddenly the door opened, and a voice said:

"I have come for you, clothes!"

At once the clean, dry, mangled,

ironed clothes made neat piles by the door – and on top poor Busy-Body was flung, wet and dripping!

"Good gracious! What's this?" said Madam Soapsuds, in surprise. "You, Busy-Body! Serves you right for peeping and prying. You're not dry, mangled or ironed. Go back and be done properly."

"No, no!" squealed Busy-Body, afraid. "Let me go. Let me go!" Madam Soapsuds got hold of him.

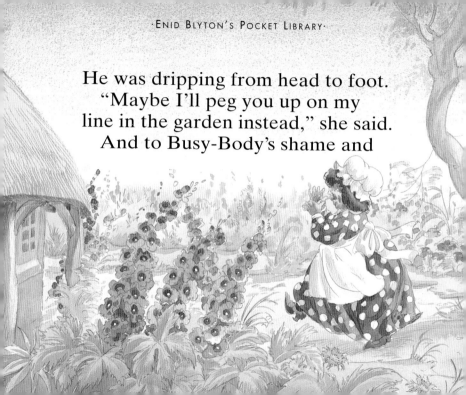

He was dripping from head to foot. "Maybe I'll peg you up on my line in the garden instead," she said. And to Busy-Body's shame and

horror, she pegged him firmly up on
her clothes line by the seat of his
trousers – and there he swung in the
wind, unable to get away.

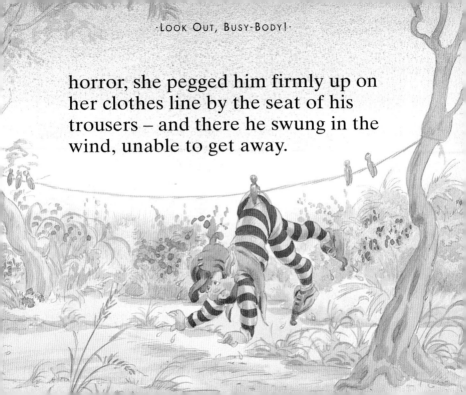

Everyone came to look and laugh.
"He poked his nose into what
didn't concern him," said Madam
Soapsuds. "He's got a lot of secrets
to tell. But if he tells them he'll go
back into my Washing Room to learn
a few more!"

Busy-Body was so ashamed and
unhappy that he cried tears into the
puddle made by his dripping clothes.
Nobody felt very sorry for him.
Busybodies are always punished by

themselves in the end!

"Now you can go," said Madam
Soapsuds, at last, unpegging him.
"And what are you going to do,
Busy-Body? Are you going to run
round telling my secrets?"

No. Busy-Body wasn't going to
do anything of the sort. He didn't
even want to think of that awful
Washing Room. So he tried not to.

But he can't help dreaming about
it, and when the neighbours hear

him yelling at night, they laugh and say: "He thinks he's in that Washing Room again. Poor Busy-Body!"